DINOSAUR WOODS

Can Seven Clever Critters Save Their Forest Home?

by
George
McClements

Beach Lane Books

New York London Toronto Sydney

For my pack:
Rachel,
Samuel,
and Matthew

FUTURE HOME OF ANOTHER
**PLAS-TIC
TREES
FACTORY**
CLEARING STARTS IN 4 DAYS

In four days, seven friends were going to lose their home.

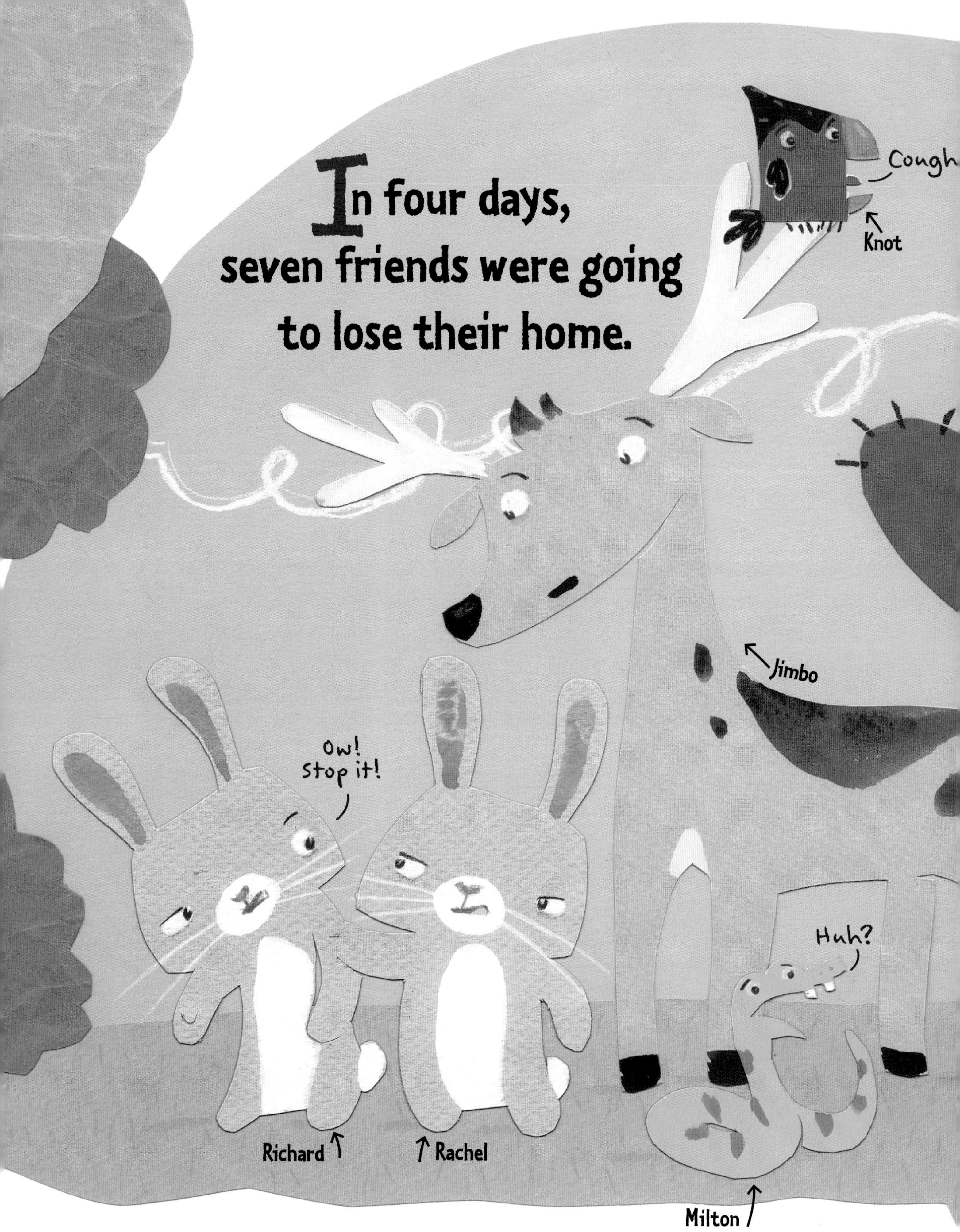

They tried to speak to the people responsible.

But for some reason, no one would listen.

"I know," said Rojo. "But we can't give up.
We need something new.
Something **BIG.**
Something AMAZING."

So the friends started thinking.

And thinking.

And thinking.

Until Rojo was struck by an idea.

(Actually, it was a piece of paper.)

Come see the

AMAZING DINOSAURS

LIFELIKE ROBOTICS

"Truly the most special animals to have walked the Earth." -Paul Leon Tologist, MESOZOIC MAGAZINE

"They're the cat's meow!" -Hey Daddyo, OLD SLANG WEEKLY

"These dinosaurs will surely add some pizzazz to your day." -Snappy Fingers, THE LOUNGE SINGER TIMES

ONLY AT THE BIG-TIME CONVENTION CENTER

"That's it!" he cried.

"We'll build a dinosaur!

There's no way they'll tear down our home

if they think a dinosaur lives here!"

Everyone agreed.

The friends spent the rest of the day collecting materials.

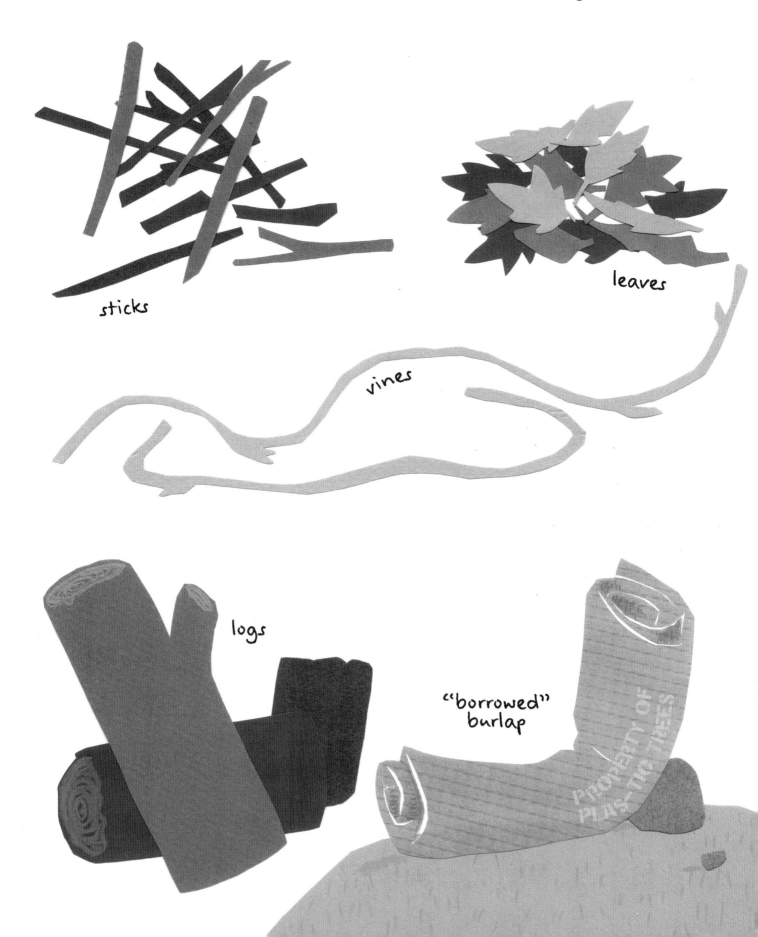

sticks

leaves

vines

logs

"borrowed" burlap

PROPERTY OF PLAS-TIC TUBES

Then Rojo spent the next thirty-six hours working in total secrecy, until . . .

. . . the dinosaur was finished.

"How does it work?"
asked Jimbo.

"It's easy," said Rojo. "First, we climb in.

Second, we take our preassigned stations.

And third, we scare away the guys on the bulldozers."

"Look!" said Luke. "Someone's coming!"

Two men making their final demolition check entered the clearing.

"Quick! Everyone to your stations!" shouted Rojo.

Rojo took a deep breath. He crossed his fingers.

And then he roared a terrible **roar.**

It worked!
The men ran for their lives.

As word of the dinosaur spread, scientists and news crews from around the world flocked to the tiny patch of woods.

"This is great!" said Rojo. "Nothing can go wrong now."

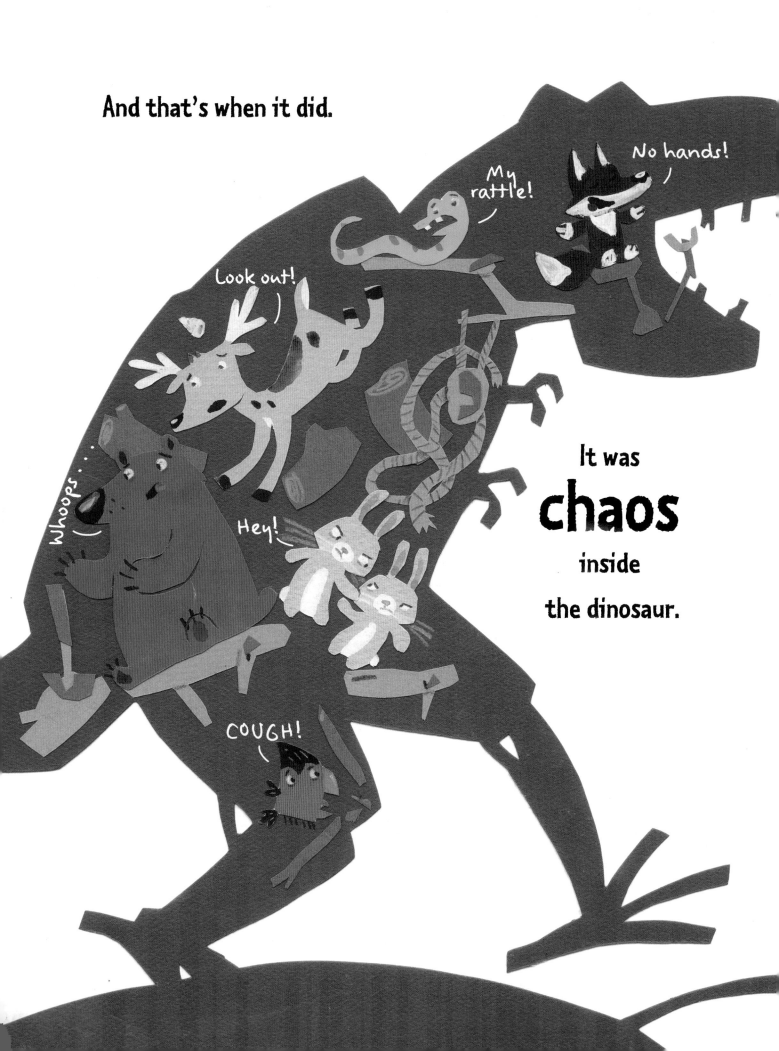

But the biggest problem? That came when
Rojo failed to notice a cable on the ground.

biggest problem

When the dust cleared,
the friends found themselves
surrounded by cameras
and clipboards.

"Get ready for some shouting," said Rojo.

And he was right.

There **was** shouting—**excited** shouting!

"A Big-Mouth Jinx Fox!"

"A Bronchial Woodpecker!"

Cough.

"A Himalayan Frost Bear!"

It turned out that the friends were something called **endangered** and, in Milton's case, *extinct*.

An important scientist declared the tiny patch of woods a protected site. And she named it Dinosaur Woods.

EU GABBIUS MAXIMUS BLAH BLAH BLAH

So, in the end, the small group of friends *did* have something to save their home.

It wasn't new.
It wasn't big.
But it **was** amazing.

They
had
each
other.

Build Your Own DINOSAUR!

(No power tools necessary.)

① Find some interesting paper.

Hint: Check the recycling bin!

newspaper

wrapping paper

brown paper bag

sandpaper

② Sketch a dinosaur, any kind you want—or try the one from the book. But don't draw the legs. (That part comes later.)

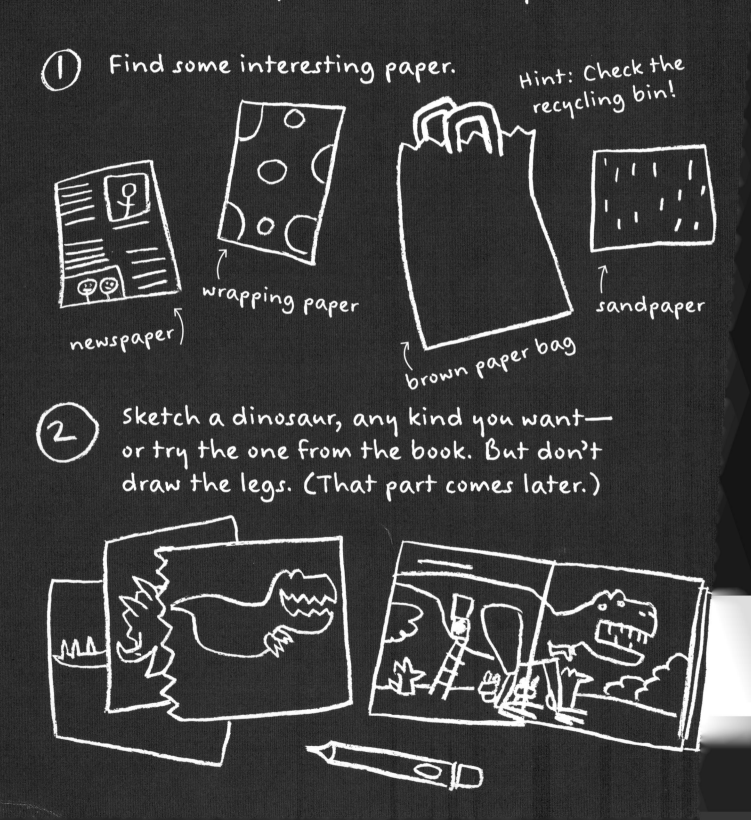

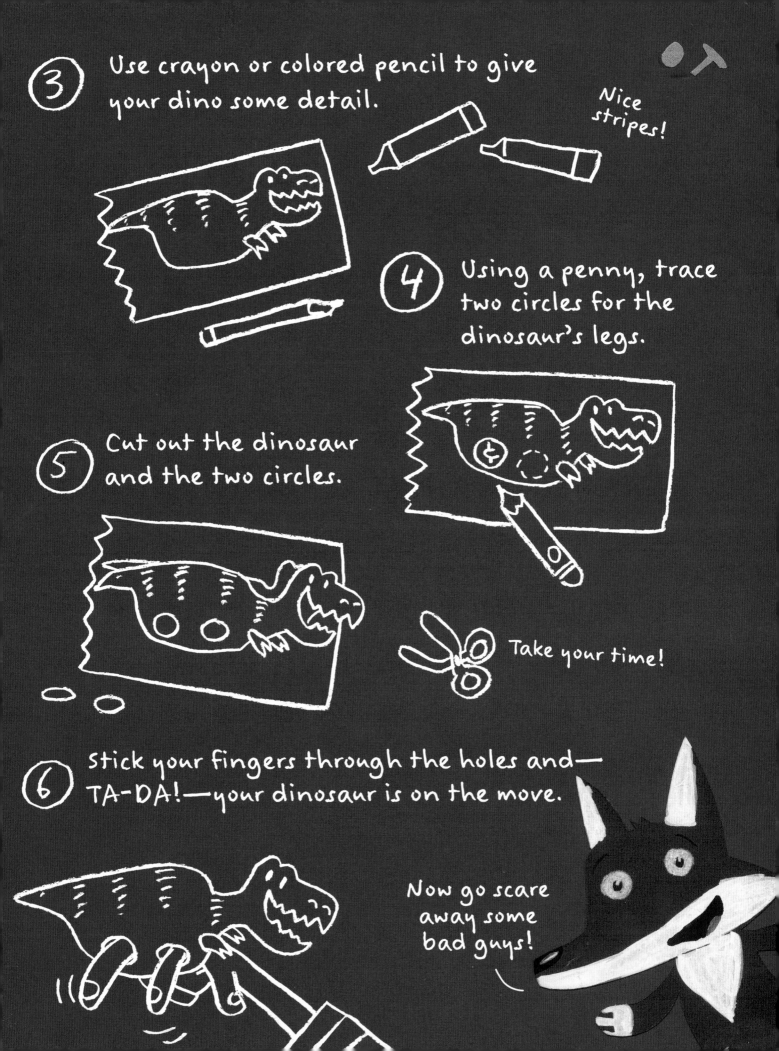

③ Use crayon or colored pencil to give your dino some detail.

Nice stripes!

④ Using a penny, trace two circles for the dinosaur's legs.

⑤ Cut out the dinosaur and the two circles.

Take your time!

⑥ Stick your fingers through the holes and—TA-DA!—your dinosaur is on the move.

Now go scare away some bad guys!

Special thanks to Andrea, Allyn, Linda, and Lauren

BEACH LANE BOOKS

An imprint of Simon & Schuster Children's Publishing Division

1230 Avenue of the Americas, New York, New York 10020

Copyright © 2009 by George McClements

Book design by Lauren Rille

The text for this book is set in Kosmik and Felt Tip Woman.

The illustrations for this book are rendered
in mixed-media collage.

Manufactured in China

First Edition

2 4 6 8 10 9 7 5 3 1

Library of Congress Cataloging-in-Publication Data

McClements, George.

Dinosaur Woods : can seven clever critters save their forest home? / George McClements. — 1st ed.

p. cm.

Summary: To save their homes from being destroyed by developers,
a fanciful group of endangered animals construct a fearsome dinosaur.

ISBN: 978-1-4169-8626-3

[1. Endangered species—Fiction. 2. Animals—Fiction. 3. Dinosaurs—Fiction.
4. Environmental protection—Fiction.] I. Title.

PZ7.M1325Di 2009

[E]—dc22

2008033084